One Giant Leap

CHARACTERS

Narrator

Jane Wilson

Pete Brooks

Dr. Vargas

Mission Control
Expert 1

Todd

Mission Control
Expert 2

Amanda

Mike Collins

Emma

Neil Armstrong

Buzz Aldrin

SETTING

NASA Mission Control Center,
Houston, Texas, 1969

Narrator: On July 20, 1969, humans walked on the surface of the Moon for the very first time. Black-and-white images of the Moon's surface flashed on television screens everywhere. The whole world was watching. Let's journey back to that time for a firsthand account of that historic event.

Jane Wilson: This is Jane Wilson, reporting live from the Mission Control Center in Houston. As you know, four days ago, on July 16, the Apollo mission lifted off from Cape Canaveral, Florida. The three astronauts on board have traveled 240,000 miles, or 400,000 kilometers, to the Moon. In just minutes they will attempt the first Moon landing. Their spacecraft has separated into two parts: the command module *Columbia* and the lunar module *Eagle*. *Columbia* is piloted by Mike Collins. It will orbit the Moon while *Eagle*, piloted by Neil Armstrong and Buzz Aldrin, makes the historic landing. Let's go to Pete Brooks in the studio for a historical perspective.

Pete Brooks: Thanks, Jane. I'm here with Dr. Vargas. He is an expert on the history of the United States space program. Dr. Vargas, why is this mission so important?

Dr. Vargas: For years, Pete, the United States competed with Russia to have the best space program. It all started on October 4, 1957, when the Russians launched *Sputnik*, the first satellite. Then, on April 12, 1961, Yuri Gagarin, a Soviet cosmonaut, became the first person in space.

Pete Brooks: Americans were taken by surprise?

Dr. Vargas: Absolutely. They felt defeated.

Pete Brooks: What turned things around for the U.S.?

Dr. Vargas: In 1961, President Kennedy challenged us to put a person on the Moon by 1970. And today the world is witnessing our effort to fulfill that challenge.

Pete Brooks: Thank you, Dr. Vargas. Now let's go back to Mission Control and Jane Wilson. Jane, are you there?

Jane Wilson: I am, Pete. The Command Center at Houston is a huge room filled with workstations. At many of these stations, Mission Control experts monitor important data coming from the *Apollo 11* spacecraft. You can feel the tension in this room. Right now I am standing with some very special visitors. With me is astronaut Mike Collins' wife, Emma, and their two children, Todd and Amanda. We are joined by two Mission Control experts. Can you tell us what is happening now?

Mission Control Expert 1: We're standing in our communications area. This is where we monitor the instruments on *Columbia* and *Eagle*.

Todd: Wow, I've never seen so many computers in one place!

Mission Control Expert 2: If you think these are impressive, you should see the *Columbia* command module. That's where your dad is now. Behind the command module is the service module. That's the part of the ship that holds fuel, oxygen, and navigational equipment.

Amanda: We're really proud of our dad.

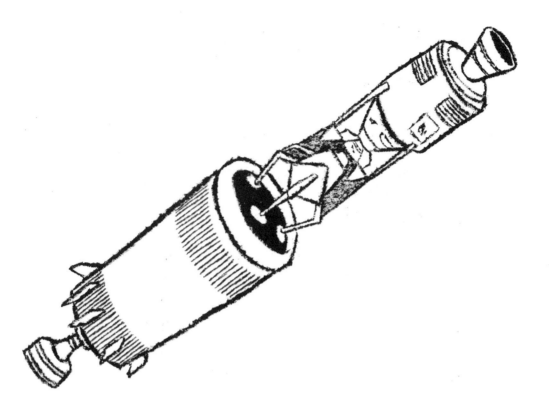

Mission Control Expert 1: Would you like to speak to him now? We have *Columbia* on our radio. Here, say hello.

Amanda and **Todd:** Hi, Dad!

Mike Collins: Hi, kids!

Todd: I wish we had a telescope that could let us see him.

Emma: Todd, the most powerful telescope in the world couldn't see something as small as the *Columbia.* It's too far away.

Mission Control Expert 1: Your mom's right. Think of how far away your father is. His rocket goes 24,000 miles per hour, and it still took him two days to get to the Moon.

Todd: My dad went 24,000 miles per hour?

Mission Control Expert 2: That's right. And do you know why? There's no air and very little gravity in space, so you can travel very fast. Newton's first law of motion states that once you are moving, you won't stop or change direction unless a force acts on you. In a car, friction with the ground constantly slows you down. In an airplane, air resistance works against forward motion. But in space there's nothing to stop you!

Todd: But because there's air and gravity on Earth, it took tons of fuel to lift off, right?

Mission Control Expert 1: Right. Remember, the rocket that launched this mission had three stages. The first stage had seven and one-half million pounds of thrust. That's a lot of power. The rocket pushed off the ground on a jet of super-heated gas. The second stage needed less than half the power, because the rocket was lighter after all that fuel burned off. The third stage was the smallest, even though it carried the astronauts the farthest.

Todd: But if there's no air to push against in space, how does the rocket move forward?

Mission Control Expert 2: Good question. That's Newton's second law of motion—every action has an equal and opposite reaction. When the exhaust gases leave the rocket, they push back and the rocket moves forward. On lift-off, the force of the exhaust gases moving down propels the rocket in the opposite direction— up—with the same force.

Amanda: Dad, are you still there? What did it feel like during liftoff? We were three miles away, and we felt the ground shake.

Mike Collins: It squashed us in our seats until we could barely breathe. It added "Gs," or gravitational forces. Right now, Amanda, you feel one G. On liftoff we felt three Gs. It was like being at the bottom curve of a roller coaster.

Todd: Cool!

Mission Control Expert 2: You need all that thrust at liftoff because the rocket is so heavy.

Amanda: But it weighs almost nothing in space, right?

Mission Control Expert 1: If your dad wanted to, he could push the ship with his hands.

Emma: That's pretty amazing, isn't it, Amanda?

Amanda: Mom, didn't you say Buzz and Neil won't weigh much on the Moon?

Emma: Yes, I did, Amanda.

Mission Control Expert 2: Your mom's right. Another one of Newton's laws says that gravity attracts all masses to one another. And the greater the mass, the greater the gravity. The Moon's mass is about $1/80$ the mass of Earth. Its gravity is about one-sixth the gravity of Earth. On Earth, the two astronauts who will walk on the Moon each weigh 360 pounds with their space suits on. On the Moon they weigh only 60—

Mission Control Expert 1: I'm sorry, but I have to interrupt you now. We have the lunar module on the line. Neil, what is your status?

Neil Armstrong: We're approaching the landing site. It looks pretty rocky. I'll keep moving to see if I can find a smoother spot.

Jane Wilson: This is Jane Wilson reporting. For those of you who just joined us, we are here live at the Mission Control Center in Houston. Neil Armstrong and Buzz Aldrin are about to touch down on the Moon in the lunar module. In just moments, if all goes well, they will step into the vacuum of space, relying on their space suits to protect them from the harsh conditions. In case you are wondering, the Moon can be a scorching 243 degrees Fahrenheit during the lunar day and a frigid 279 degrees below zero Fahrenheit during the lunar night.

Mission Control Expert 1: *Eagle*, this is Mission Control. You'll have to set down soon. You're low on fuel.

Neil Armstrong: Roger, Mission Control. We've found a landing spot.

Todd: What happens if they crash?

Mission Control Expert 2: The *Eagle* is moving very slowly. A crash would probably only break the legs. The section with the legs remains on the Moon after liftoff.

Jane Wilson: There's absolute quiet here at the Mission Control Center as everyone waits.

Neil Armstrong: Mission Control, this is Tranquility base here. The *Eagle* has landed.

Jane Wilson: There you have it. "The *Eagle* has landed." Those are the words of Neil Armstrong—the first words spoken from the Moon. The lunar module has just landed on the Sea of Tranquility, one of the dark areas on the Moon that is visible from Earth. The astronauts will now prepare their life-support units for the first moonwalk.

Todd: Amanda, the life-support units have oxygen tanks, water, and all the radio equipment in big backpacks.

Amanda: I know. And Dad told me the space suits cost more than $1 million each.

Todd: The Sun filters on their helmets are made of gold foil. On Earth the atmosphere blocks most of the Sun's rays, but on the Moon, the Sun would burn your skin in a few seconds. The space suits also keep the astronauts at the right temperature.

Mission Control Expert 1: You've been teaching them everything, haven't you, Mrs. Collins?

Emma: Well, this is one of the greatest scientific achievements of the century. I want them to remember everything.

Neil Armstrong: I'm ready to open the hatch now. I'm taking out the camera and turning it on.

Jane Wilson: What you now see on your television screens is live footage from the Moon.

Mission Control Expert 1: Neil will have to jump the last three feet to the ground. We had to make the ladder short to save on weight.

Emma: I can't believe this is actually happening.

Neil Armstrong: I'm stepping onto the ladder now, down to the bottom step.

Narrator: The images of Neil Armstrong climbing out of the lunar module are among the most famous in the world. His space suit was bulky, and his movements were awkward in the low-gravity environment. He stepped cautiously down the ladder, hopped off the end, and landed on the surface of the Moon. He said—

Neil Armstrong: That's one small step for a man, one giant leap for mankind.

Narrator: A few minutes later, Buzz Aldrin joined him.

Jane Wilson: The astronauts will perform several experiments on the Moon. One involves running at full speed and then trying to stop in the low-gravity environment. In the vacuum of space, the astronauts must be careful not to tear their space suits. The suits recreate the air pressure on Earth, and a loss of pressure could result in injury or death.

Neil Armstrong: This Moon dust is strange stuff. In the distance it looks white, almost blue, and in other places it seems kind of yellow. Beneath our feet it's mostly gray, but when I pick it up, it looks brown or black.

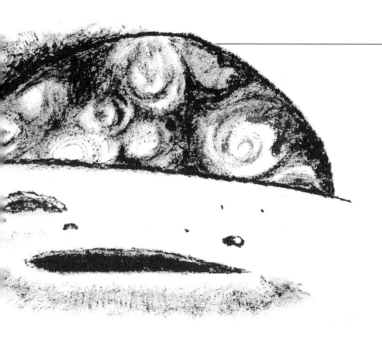

Buzz Aldrin: The horizon seems much closer here than it does on Earth—but wait, what's that I see coming up just over the hill?

Mission Control Expert 1: What are you seeing, *Eagle*?

Buzz Aldrin: It's Earth rising, like a pale sunrise in the morning. It's the most beautiful thing I've ever seen.

Jane Wilson: For the first time in history, people look at Earth from the Moon. The astronauts will place a plaque near the spot where the *Eagle* landed. The plaque reads, "Here, men from the planet Earth first set foot upon the moon, July, 1969 A.D. We came in peace for all mankind."

Narrator: Since that day, scientists have continued to explore outer space. The international space station makes it possible for humans to live in orbit for months. The Hubble telescope takes glorious photographs of stars light-years away. Probes have photographed the surfaces of almost every planet in the solar system. But no human has ever traveled farther than Neil Armstrong, Buzz Aldrin, and Mike Collins did. Even if we never travel beyond the Moon, we will always know we are not bound to Earth. We are truly ambitious explorers of the universe.

The End

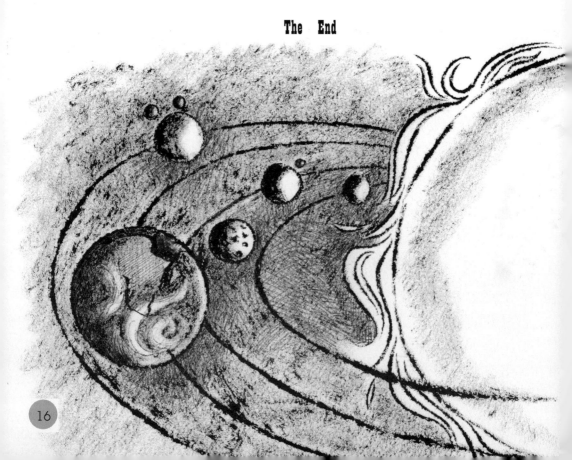